W9-CPY-120

Dear Parent:

Congratulations! Your child is taking
the first steps on an exciting journey.
The destination? Independent reading!

STEP INTO READING® will help your child get there. The program offers
five steps to reading success. Each step includes fun stories and colorful art.
There are also Step into Reading Sticker Books, Step into Reading Math
Readers, Step into Reading Phonics Readers, Step into Reading Write-In
Readers, and Step into Reading Phonics Boxed Sets—a complete literacy
program with something for every child.

Learning to Read, Step by Step!

Ready to Read   Preschool–Kindergarten
• big type and easy words • rhyme and rhythm • picture clues
For children who know the alphabet and are eager to
begin reading.

Reading with Help   Preschool–Grade 1
• basic vocabulary • short sentences • simple stories
For children who recognize familiar words and sound out
new words with help.

Reading on Your Own   Grades 1–3
• engaging characters • easy-to-follow plots • popular topics
For children who are ready to read on their own.

Reading Paragraphs   Grades 2–3
• challenging vocabulary • short paragraphs • exciting stories
For newly independent readers who read simple sentences
with confidence.

Ready for Chapters   Grades 2–4
• chapters • longer paragraphs • full-color art
For children who want to take the plunge into chapter books
but still like colorful pictures.

STEP INTO READING® is designed to give every child a successful
reading experience. The grade levels are only guides. Children can progress
through the steps at their own speed, developing confidence in their
reading, no matter what their grade.

Remember, a lifetime love of reading starts with a single step!

© 2015 Viacom International Inc. All rights reserved. Published in the United States by Random House Children's Books, a division of Random House LLC, 1745 Broadway, New York, NY 10019, and in Canada by Random House of Canada Limited, Toronto, Penguin Random House Companies. Nickelodeon, Bubble Guppies, and all related titles, logos, and characters are trademarks of Viacom International Inc.

Step into Reading, Random House, and the Random House colophon are registered trademarks of Random House LLC.

Visit us on the Web!
StepIntoReading.com
randomhouse.com/kids

Educators and librarians, for a variety of teaching tools, visit us at RHTeachersLibrarians.com

ISBN 978-0-385-38457-5 (trade) — ISBN 978-0-385-38458-2 (lib. bdg.)
Printed in the United States of America

10 9 8 7 6 5 4 3 2 1

STEP INTO READING®

STEP 2

nickelodeon

BUBBLE GUPPIES

THE BIG MAGIC SHOW!

By Josephine Nagaraj

Cover illustrated by Sue DiCicco and Steve Talkowski

Interior illustrated by MJ Illustrations

Random House 🏠 New York

Look!
The Amazing Daisy
has come to town.
She is
a magician.

Daisy does
a magic trick.
Molly and Gil
get to help!
Daisy climbs into a box.

Gil waves

a magic wand.

Molly says

a magic word.

Poof!

Daisy is gone!

Gil looks left.

Molly looks right.

Where did Daisy go?

Daisy is
behind the tree!
How did
she get there?

Daisy climbed
out of the box.

What a good
magic trick!

Molly wants
to do magic
just like Daisy.
What does she need?

Molly needs

a magic wand.

She needs

a magic hat.

Molly needs to say
the magic word.

Magic is not easy.

It takes practice.

The big magic show
is tonight!

MAGIC
SHOW
TONIGHT

The lights are bright.

The crowd cheers.

Molly brings
an elephant onstage.
She needs to make
the elephant disappear.

It is a big trick.
Can Molly do it?

Molly has an idea.

There is

a secret door

in the floor.

Gil will press
a button.

The elephant will go
into the secret door.
Poof!

Molly waves a wand.

She says

the magic word.

Ta-da!

Molly did it!

The elephant is gone.

Magic is easy after all!